Funny Bone Readers™

Bullies Can Change

BEAR'S BAD DAY

by Wiley Blevins

illustrated by Dave Clegg

**RED
CHAIR**
•PRESS•

Please visit our website at **www.redchairpress.com**.
Find a free catalog of all our high-quality products for young readers.

Publisher's Cataloging-In-Publication Data
(Prepared by The Donohue Group, Inc.)

Blevins, Wiley.
    Bear's bad day : bullies can change / by Wiley Blevins ; illustrated by Dave Clegg.
-- [First edition].

    pages : illustrations ; cm. -- (Funny bone readers. Dealing with bullies)

    Summary: When Bear goes out in the forest to find friends, he is gruff and offends
everyone he meets-- until Bird points out that Bear is being a bully. Bear realizes he was
feeling unsure of himself so he apologizes. After that, Bear has plenty of new friends.
Includes glossary, as well as questions to self-check comprehension.
    Interest age level: 004-008.
    Edition statement supplied by publisher.
    Issued also as an ebook.
    ISBN: 978-1-63440-012-1 (library hardcover)
    ISBN: 978-1-63440-013-8 (paperback)

    1. Bears--Juvenile fiction. 2. Bullying--Juvenile fiction. 3. Friendship--Juvenile
fiction. 4. Change (Psychology)--Juvenile fiction. 5. Bears--Fiction. 6. Bullying--Fiction.
7. Friendship--Fiction. 8. Change (Psychology)--Fiction.   I. Clegg, Dave. II. Title.

PZ7.B618652 Be 2015
[E]   2014958267

This series first published by:
Red Chair Press LLC   PO Box 333   South Egremont, MA 01258-0333

Printed in the United States of America

042015 1P WRZF15

Bear lived in a cave.
In the middle of the forest.
All alone.

What Bear needed most was a friend.
So, he went out to find one.

Bear spotted Owl.
"Ha, ha!" said Bear.
"You have big, bug eyes."

"Hoo?" said Owl.
"You," said Bear.
"Hoo? Hoo?" said Owl.
"You! You!" said Bear.
"Hoo, hoo, hoot," said Owl.

"Oh never mind," said Bear.
And he walked on.

Next, Bear met Skunk.
"Wow," said Bear. "You stink."
"Thank you," said Skunk.
"That's what I was trying for."

Skunk turned around.
He lifted his tail.
1 . . . 2 . . . 3 . . .
Bear ran away.

9

As Bear was running, he saw Turtle.
"Get out of my way slowpoke,"
he growled.

"Are you having a bad day?"
asked Turtle.
Bear huffed and ran on.

After that, Bear saw Deer.
"Look at those skinny legs," he said.
"You should be called stick-legs."

"Stop it!" said Deer. "That's not nice."
"Let's get out of here," said Rabbit.

They hopped, hopped, and leaped away.

Finally, Bear walked to a river.
He sat and held his head low.
"There are no friends in this forest,"
he grumbled.

Bird flew down beside Bear.
"If you want a friend," she said,
"you have to stop being mean."

"Mean?" asked Bear.
"Yes," said Bird.
"You are a big bully!"

"I think they would make fun of me,"
said Bear. "My big belly. My hairy arms."
Bird shook her head "no."
"So what should I do?" asked Bear.

"I have an idea," said Bird.
She whispered in Bear's ear.
Bear raced back to his cave.
Bird flew to all the animals.
She told them Bear had a surprise.

When the animals got to Bear's cave, they found food, games, and a big sign. On it were written two important words.

From that day on, Bear had many friends.

Big Questions: Why was Bear being mean to the others? Was Bear acting like a bully? Why was Bear sad when Bird talked to him? What did Bear do to gain new friends?

Big Words:

bully: a person who harms others with mean words or actions